Hymns to the Night

NOVALIS

Hymns to the Night

TRANSLATED BY DICK HIGGINS

Third Edition

McPherson & Company

All rights reserved. For information, address the publisher, McPherson & Company, P.O. Box 1126, Kingston, New York 12401. Publication of this book was originally assisted by a grant from the New York State Council on the Arts. Design by Bruce R. McPherson. Manufactured in the United States of America.

Third Edition.

Library of Congress Cataloging in Publication Data

Novalis, 1772-1801.
   Hymns to the night.

   Translation of: Hymnen an die Nacht.
   English and German.
   I. Higgins, Dick, 1938-   .II. Title.
PT2291.H6E55   1988   831'.6   87-34706
ISBN 0-914232-90-8

Typeset by Winer Graphics and Open Studio Ltd. Printed and bound by McNaughton & Gunn Lithographers. The paper is acid-free.

FOREWORD

The *Hymnen an die Nacht* of "Novalis," nom de plume of George Friedrich Philip, Freiherr von Hardenberg (1772-1801), has long been recognized as one of the masterpieces of the first, Jena phase of German romanticism. The sections in free verse are highly original, while the syncretic use of myth in the fifth section, which refers to the myth of the lost golden age in Hesiod's *Cosmogony* but also blends it with the stories of the nativity, death and resurrection of Jesus Christ, has a more distinctly modern or even postmodern flavor, in that the key points of the stories are evoked and alluded to rather than stated in sequence.

Hymns to the Night first appeared in *Athenaeum* 3, n. 2 (1800), pp. 188-204—a literary magazine edited by August Wilhelm Schlegel and his brother Friedrich Schlegel, now usually spelled "Athenäum." The mixture of prose and verse in the poem epitomizes the Schlegel brothers' call against the puristic "unities" of the neo-classic period preceding it. The work was recognized as an extraordinary piece from its first publication, as a key work in establishing what became known as the romantic aesthetic, and, while not much imitated in its immediate time, still its resonances are felt throughout not only nineteenth century German literature, from early Heine to Nietzsche, but in English literature in such works as De Quincey's *Suspiria de Profundis* or Swinburne's more visionary poems.

However, the language of *Hymns to the Night* is extremely difficult, with neologisms, highly idiosyncratic word uses and involuted grammar. To an English-speaking reader, perhaps the most comparable style would be that of William Blake in the prophecies. But, unlike Blake, there is nothing archaic in Novalis' language; it is in the most resolutely modernist style of its time. It is a mistake, therefore, to translate Novalis, as has usually been done, into archaic or overly poetic English. This was, after all, the period of the great translations of Shakespeare into German. The romantics saw Shakespeare, who also mixes prose and poetry in his dramas, as a paradigm for their own reaction against French neo-classic influence, and they made of Shakespeare a then-modern German, so much so that Ludwig Tieck

referred to him as "unser William," *our* William. In much the same spirit I have translated Novalis into something approximating modern English but with occasional neologistic resonances, except where this would create a real distortion. For example, I translate Novalis' "kindlichsten" as "childlikest," because to say "most childlike" loses a tone he evokes. To offer an extreme example, from the first section, paragraph three, Powell Spring's translation reads: "Just what is it we sense so poignantly below the heart, absorbing the zephyr of sadness, soft as a prevailing breeze? Are you pleased with us, darksome night?... You brace the wings of our sentient being..." Frankly, that is mush, unjustified by Novalis' original. My own, more literal rendering of the same passage is, I hope, more subtly poetic: "What wells up so menacingly under the heart and gulps down the soft air's sadness? Are you pleased with us, dark Night?...You raise up the soul's heavy wings..."

There are two basic versions of the German text: an early manuscript version, and the *Athenäum* version based on a manuscript now lost. The surviving manuscript differs from the *Athenäum* text by being almost entirely in verse and unbroken into sections. Further, there are sharp differences in the two versions of the first hymn, enough so that we have appended this section to our text. The differences in the later portions are somewhat less, consisting of section summaries in the manuscript version which do not appear in the *Athenäum* one, and of punctuation differences, but seldom differences of actual wording. Readers who wish to pursue this matter more deeply should consult Heinz Ritter *Novalis' Hymnen an die Nacht* (Heidelberg: Carl Winter, 1974), especially the comparison of the two versions on pp. 115-40, but also the manuscript transcription on pp. 22-88 and the holograph of the manuscript, facing page 308. Our own text is the same as that which appeared in the *Athenäum,* except that spelling has been modernized ("Heimat" for "Heymath," "Tiere" for "Thiere," and so on), to avoid confusing American readers.

My work was begun in Barton, Vermont, in the summer of 1976 and finished at the Center for Twentieth Century Studies of the University of Wisconsin at Milwaukee; it was first published by

Treacle Press in 1978. That edition did not include either German text, and it therefore encountered some resistance, especially from those who did not realize the differences among these. In a few cases, however, the objections were appropriate, and I am thankful for the opportunity to correct them. I also realized that in section five, where I had formerly used only lower case initials, it seemed as if the singer who hails the birth of Jesus might be the one who was crucified and resurrected, so it is a relief to me to have the chance to clear up that potential misunderstanding.

Finally, I am very grateful to Mr. David Rattray for his observations and suggestions, and to Mr. Bruce McPherson, whose patience and proofreading skills have exceeded my own, and without whom this book would, simply, not exist.   7. *February, 1984*

Foreword to the Third Edition

So what does one do when the translation of an impossible-to-translate text, this one, which never fails to fascinate anew, is offered a third edition? In this case I took out my folder of reviews, chose the two most negative ones, and considered whether there was truth in their criticisms. I concluded there was, and wrote to their authors. Professors Paul Webster, of the Department of Languages, Pacific Lutheran University, Tacoma, Washington, and Arthur Alt, of the German Department, Duke University, Durham, North Carolina, both wrote back with many positive suggestions. This led me to some fairly extensive revisions of the actual readings, if not of the diction which I had worked out earlier as being relatively suitable for Novalis in English. The result is a text which I am prepared to put to bed. Gone is "earthy" for "irdisch," borrowed from Novalis' near-contemporary Keats, who sometimes uses the term to mean "worldly" or "earthly"; our modern usage of the term is simply too far from Keats's. Professor Alt stressed Novalis' training as a mining engineer, suggesting detailed revisions which reflect this. Professor Webster stressed eighteenth century usages which I had not known: "ahnden" for "ahnen" on page 51, for example. To both of these scholars I am deeply thankful.

Professor Webster also called my attention to the passage on page 29, the puzzling passage which reads: "The orient's portentous, rich-blooming wisdom was the first to recognize the beginning of the new time..." He pointed out that this is a reference to the Wise Men who came to adore the infant Jesus, as is borne out a few lines later. It would have been very tempting, therefore, to substitute some word like "adept" for "wisdom," to avoid the awkward personification. But it would not be what Novalis said. He also drew my attention to the difficulties of translating "Schoß," literally "lap," as in the final word of the poem, because it carries those associations which we make with "womb" or even "bosom." I have decided not to be consistent in using any *single* word to render "Schoß," believing no single English word fits the many uses in the *Hymns*.

Professor Alt called my attention to several errors in the German texts I was using (as well as to a few simple typographic errors in mine, now corrected); but all I could do here was to establish a working consensus among the German versions at my reach. A few problem passages remain nonetheless: on page 40, one must choose between "deucht," the more modern word, and "däucht." It is impossible to tell which would be better.

In the translation itself, in the opening section on page 11, "Down over there, far, lies the world..." is more awkward than "Fernab liegt die Welt," but my earlier version, "Over there, far, lies the world," lacks the downward sense necessary to suggest the grave, the image which dominates the passage. And in section four, page 20, there is no simple English word corresponding to "wallen," meaning "to go on a pilgrimage." I chose "quest," but it is inadequate; still, to use the longer, more accurate phrase would have broken the simplicity of the lines. Finally, four lines further, it is hard to determine just how to translate "Noch wenig Zeiten..." "Zeiten" would normally be the plural of "time," but it also could be "seasons" (with all the metaphorical associations of that word) as well as "moments." There is no single correct translation possible here.

Once again, I repeat my thanks to Professors Webster and Alt, who so clearly share my love of Novalis' *Hymnen an die Nacht*.

17. August, 1987

Hymns to the Night

1

Welcher Lebendige, Sinnbegabte, liebt nicht vor allen Wundererscheinungen des verbreiteten Raums um ihn, das allerfreuliche Licht — mit seinen Farben, seinen Strahlen und Wogen; seiner milden Allgegenwart, als weckender Tag. Wie des Lebens innerste Seele atmet es der rastlosen Gestirne Riesenwelt, und schwimmt tanzend in seiner blauen Flut — atmet es der funkelnde, ewigruhende Stein, die sinnige, saugende Pflanze, und das wilde, brennende, vielgestaltete Tier — vor allen aber der herrliche Fremdling mit den sinnvollen Augen, dem schwebenden Gange, und den zartgeschlossenen, tonreichen Lippen. Wie ein König der irdischen Natur ruft es jede Kraft zu zahllosen Verwandlungen, knüpft und löst unendliche Bündnisse, hängt sein himmlisches Bild jedem irdischen Wesen um. —Seine Gegenwart allein offenbart die Wunderherrlichkeit der Reiche der Welt.

Abwärts wend ich mich zu der heiligen, unaussprechlichen, geheimnisvollen Nacht. Fernab liegt die Welt — in eine tiefe Gruft versenkt—wüst und einsam ist ihre Stelle. In den Saiten der Brust weht tiefe Wehmut. In Tautropfen will ich hinuntersinken und mit der Asche mich vermischen. —Fernen der Erinnerung, Wünsche der Jugend, der Kindheit Träume, des ganzen langen Lebens kurze Freuden und vergebliche Hoffnungen kommen in grauen Kleidern, wie Abendnebel nach der Sonne Untergang. In andern Räumen schlug die lustigen Gezelte das Licht auf. Sollte es nie zu seinen Kindern wiederkommen, die mit der Unschuld Glauben seiner harren?

Was quillt auf einmal so ahndungsvoll unterm Herzen, und verschluckt der Wehmut weiche Luft? Hast auch du ein Gefallen an uns, dunkle Nacht? Was hältst du unter deinem Mantel, das mir unsichtbar kräftig an die Seele geht? Köstlicher Balsam träuft

1

What living person, gifted with any sense, doesn't love, more than all the wonderful appearances of spread-out space around him, the all-joyful Light—with its colors, beams, waves; its gentle presence, as waking day. As life's inner soul it's breathed by the Giant-world of restless stars, and swims dancing in its blue tide—the glittering, ever-peaceful stone breathes it, the sensuous sucking plant, the wild and burning so many formed beast—but above all that splendid stranger with sense-filled eyes, with gliding gait and gently-closed, rich-toned lips. Like an earthly nature king, it summons each force to uncounted changes, makes and dissolves each force joinings without end, hangs its heavenly picture on each earthly being.—Its presence alone opens up the wonder, the splendor of the earth's kingdoms.

Away I turn to the holy, the unspeakable, the secretive Night. Down over there, far, lies the world—sunken in a deep vault—its place wasted and lonely. In the heart's strings, deep sadness blows. In dewdrops I'll sink and mix with the ashes. —Memory's distances, youth's wishes, childhood's dreams, the short joys of a whole long life and hopeless hopes come grey-clad, like evening mist after the sun has set. In other places Light's pitched happy tents. Should It never come back to Its children, who are waiting for it with simple faith?

What wells up so menacingly under the heart and gulps down the soft air's sadness? Are you pleased with us, dark Night? What're you holding under your cloak, that grabs so unseen at my soul? Costly balm drips from your hand, from a bundle of poppies. You raise up the soul's heavy wings. Darkly, unspeakably we feel moved—I see a serious face startled with

aus deiner Hand, aus dem Bündel Mohn. Die schweren Flügel des Gemüts hebst du empor. Dunkel und unaussprechlich fühlen wir uns bewegt — ein ernstes Antlitz seh ich froh erschrocken, das sanft und andachtsvoll sich zu mir neigt, und unter unendlich verschlungenen Locken der Mutter liebe Jugend zeigt. Wie arm und kindisch dünkt mir das Licht nun — wie erfreulich und gesegnet des Tages Abschied — Also nur darum, weil die Nacht dir abwendig macht die Dienenden, säetest du in des Raumes Weiten die leuchtenden Kugeln, zu verkünden deine Allmacht — deine Wiederkehr — in den Zeiten deiner Entfernung. Himmlischer, als jene blitzenden Sterne, dünken uns die unendlichen Augen, die die Nacht in uns geöffnet. Weiter sehn sie, als die blässesten jener zahllosen Heere — unbedürftig des Lichts durchschaun sie die Tiefen eines liebenden Gemüts — was einen höhern Raum mit unsäglicher Wollust füllt. Preis der Weltkönigin, der hohen Verkündigerin heiliger Welten, der Pflegerin seliger Liebe — sie sendet mir dich — zarte Geliebte — liebliche Sonne der Nacht, — nun wach ich — denn ich bin Dein und Mein — du hast die Nacht mir zum Leben verkündet — mich zum Menschen gemacht — zehre mit Geisterglut meinen Leib, daß ich luftig mit dir inniger mich mische und dann ewig die Brautnacht währt.

joy, it bends to me softly, reverently, and under the endlessly tangled locks of the Mother's dear youth shows. How poor and childish the Light seems now—how happy and blessed the day's departure—So now, since Night turns your servants away from you, you'd sow gleaming spheres in the far spaces to show your own omnipotence—your return—in the times of your distance. More heavenly than those flashing stars the endless eyes seem, which Night opens up in us. They see farther than those palest of those countless hosts—having no need for Light they see through the depths of a loving soul—which fills a higher space with unspeakable delight. Praise the world queen, the higher messenger of a holy word, a nurse of blessed love—she sends you—tender, beloved—Night's lovely sun,—now, I wake—for I'm yours and mine—you called the Night to life for me,—humanized me—consume my body with spirit fire, so I can mix with you more intimately, airily, and then the wedding night will last forever.

2

Muß immer der Morgen wiederkommen? Endet nie des Irdischen Gewalt? unselige Geschäftigkeit verzehrt den himmlischen Anflug der Nacht. Wird nie der Liebe geheimes Opfer ewig brennen? Zugemessen ward dem Lichte seine Zeit; aber zeitlos und raumlos ist der Nacht Herrschaft. — Ewig ist die Dauer des Schlafs. Heiliger Schlaf—beglücke zu selten nicht der Nacht Geweihte in diesem irdischen Tagewerk. Nur die Toren verkennen dich und wissen von keinem Schlafe, als dem Schatten, den du in jener Dämmerung der wahrhaften Nacht mitleidig auf uns wirfst. Sie fühlen dich nicht in der goldnen Flut der Trauben — in des Mandelbaums Wunderöl, und dem braunen Safte des Mohns. Sie wissen nicht, daß du es bist, der des zarten Mädchens Busen umschwebt und zum Himmel den Schoß macht—ahnden nicht, daß aus alten Geschichten du himmelöffnend entgegentrittst und den Schlüssel trägst zu den Wohnungen der Seligen, unendlicher Geheimnisse schweigender Bote.

2

Must the morning always return? Will earthly force never end? Unholy busyness devours the Night's heavenward approach. Won't Love's secret offering ever burn forever? Light's time was measured out to it; but Night's reign is timeless and spaceless. —Forever's the length of sleep. Holy sleep—don't make Night's elect too rarely happy in this earthly day-labor. Only fools misrecognize you and know no sleep but the shadow which, in that twilight before the true Night, you, pitying, throw over us. They don't feel you in the grapes' golden flood—in almond trees' wonder oil—in poppies' brown juice. They don't know it's you hovering around a tender girl's breasts making her womb heaven—and don't suspect that, out of old stories, you, opening heaven up, come and carry the key to the Dwellings of the Blessed, quiet messenger of infinite mysteries.

3

Einst da ich bittre Tränen vergoß, da in Schmerz aufgelöst
meine Hoffnung zerrann, und ich einsam stand am dürren Hügel,
der in engen, dunklen Raum die Gestalt meines Lebens barg—
einsam, wie noch kein Einsamer war, von unsäglicher Angst ge-
trieben—kraftlos, nur ein Gedanken des Elends noch. —Wie ich
da nach Hülfe umherschaute, vorwärts nicht konnte und rück-
wärts nicht, und am fliehenden, verlöschten Leben mit unendlicher Sehnsucht hing: —da kam aus blauen Fernen—von den
Höhen meiner alten Seligkeit ein Dämmerungsschauer—und mit
einem Male riß das Band der Geburt—des Lichtes Fessel. Hin
floh die irdische Herrlichkeit und meine Trauer mit ihr—zusam-
men floß die Wehmut in eine neue, unergründliche Welt—du
Nachtbegeisterung, Schlummer des Himmels kamst über mich
—die Gegend hob sich sacht empor; über der Gegend schwebte
mein entbundner, neugeborner Geist. Zur Staubwolke wurde der
Hügel—durch die Wolke sah ich die verklärten Züge der Geliebten. In ihren Augen ruhte die Ewigkeit—ich faßte ihre Hände,
und die Tränen wurden ein funkelndes, unzerreißliches Band.
Jahrtausende zogen abwärts in die Ferne, wie Ungewitter. An
ihrem Halse weint ich dem neuen Leben entzückende Tränen. —
Es war der erste, einzige Traum—und erst seitdem fühl ich ewigen,
unwandelbaren Glauben an den Himmel der Nacht und sein
Licht, die Geliebte.

3

Once, when I poured out bitter tears, when, dissolved in pain, scattered, and I was standing alone at the barren mound which hid the figure of my life in its narrow, dark space—alone, as no one could be more alone, driven by unspeakable anxiety—strengthless, with just one thought left of need. —As I looked around for help, could not move forwards and not backwards, and hung onto the fleeting, extinguished life with infinite craving:—then came from blue distances—from the heights of my old blessedness, a twilight shiver—and with one stroke my birth's bond ripped—Light's chains. There the earthly splendor fled and my sadness with it—misery flowed into a new, unplumbed world—You, Night-inspiration,* heaven's sleep, came over me—the region lifted gently up; over the region my released and newborn spirit floated. The hill became a cloud of dust—through the cloud I saw the transfigured features of my beloved. In her eyes rested the forever—I took her hands, and my tears were a glittering and unrippable bond. Years by the thousands flew off to the distance, like storms. In her embrace I wept overjoyed tears at the new life. —It was the first and the only dream—and only since then I've felt an unchangeable, eternal faith in the heaven of Night and its Light, the beloved.

---

*Some editions have "*Nach*begeisterung" here, "after-inspiration," which makes little sense. Ours says, however, "*Nacht*begeisterung," as does the original *Athenäum* version. —*D.H.*

4

Nun weiß ich, wenn der letzte Morgen sein wird—wenn das Licht nicht mehr die Nacht und die Liebe scheucht—wenn der Schlummer ewig und nur Ein unerschöpflicher Traum sein wird. Himmlische Müdigkeit fühl ich in mir. —Weit und ermüdend ward mir die Wallfahrt zum heiligen Grabe, drückend das Kreuz. Die kristallene Woge, die gemeinen Sinnen unvernehmlich, in des Hügels dunkeln Schoß quillt, an dessen Fuß die irdische Flut bricht, wer sie gekostet, wer oben stand auf dem Grenzgebürge der Welt, und hinübersah in das neue Land, in der Nacht Wohnsitz—wahrlich der kehrt nicht in das Treiben der Welt zurück, in das Land, wo das Licht in ewiger Unruh hauset.

Oben baut er sich Hütten, Hütten des Friedens, sehnt sich und liebt, schaut hinüber, bis die willkommenste aller Stunden hinunter ihn in den Brunnen der Quelle zieht — das Irdische schwimmt oben auf, wird von Stürmen zurückgeführt, aber was heilig durch der Liebe Berührung ward, rinnt aufgelöst in verborgenen Gängen auf das jenseitige Gebiet, wo es, wie Düfte, sich mit entschlummerten Lieben mischt.

Noch weckst du, muntres Licht, den Müden zur Arbeit — flößest fröhliches Leben mir ein—aber du lockst mich von der Erinnerung moosigem Denkmal nicht. Gern will ich die fleißigen Hände rühren, überall umschaun, wo du mich brauchst—rühmen deines Glanzes volle Pracht—unverdrossen verfolgen deines künstlichen Werks schönen Zusammenhang—gern betrachten deiner gewaltigen, leuchtenden Uhr sinnvollen Gang—ergründen der Kräfte Ebenmaß und die Regeln des Wunderspiels unzähliger Räume und ihrer Zeiten. Aber getreu der Nacht bleibt mein geheimes Herz, und der schaffenden Liebe, ihrer Tochter. Kannst du mir zeigen ein ewig treues Herz? hat deine Sonne freundliche

4

Now I know when the final morning will be—when the Light will no longer frighten away the Night and love—when sleeping will be forever just one unsuspendable dream. I feel heavenly tiredness in myself. Far and tiring to me this pilgrimage to the holy grave has been and the cross oppresses. The crystal wave, unnoticeable by common senses, wells up in the mound's dark womb, at the foot where the worldly tide ebbs, whoever's tasted it, whoever's stood up on the world's watershed, and looked over into the new land, into Night's dwelling—truly such a one won't come back to the world's doings, to the land where Light is housed in eternal unrest.

Up there he builds shelters, peace's shelters, longs and loves, looks over till the welcomest of all hours pulls him down into the source of sources—the worldly swells up, is led back by storms, but what became holy through the touch of love, that runs freed through hidden channels to the other side where it, like breezes, mixes with loves that have passed on to sleep.

For now, bright Light, you are waking those tired ones to work—implanting cheerful life in me—but you won't tempt me from the memory's mossy monument. I'll gladly stir my busy hands, look round where you need me—celebrate your shining's whole splendor—untiring, follow up your art's lovely consequent—gladly watch your strong, gleaming clock's sensible course—plumb strength's measure and the rules of the wonder play of countless spaces and their times. But my secret heart stays true to the Night, and to creative Love, her daughter. Can you show me a heart that stays true forever? has your sun got friendly eyes to recognize me? do your stars take my desiring hand? and return my tender touch and loving word? have you

Augen, die mich erkennen? fassen deine Sterne meine verlang-
ende Hand? geben mir wieder den zärtlichen Druck und das
kosende Wort? hast du mit Farben und leichtem Umriß sie geziert
—oder war Sie es, die deinem Schmuck höhere, liebere Bedeu-
tung gab? Welche Wollust, welchen Genuß bietet dein Leben,
die aufwögen des Todes Entzückungen? Trägt nicht alles, was uns
begeistert, die Farbe der Nacht? Sie trägt dich mütterlich und ihr
verdankst du all deine Herrlichkeit. Du verflögst in dir selbst—
in endlosen Raum zergingst du, wenn sie dich nicht hielte, dich
nicht bände, daß du warm würdest und flammend die Welt zeug-
test. Wahrlich ich war, eh du warst—die Mutter schickte mit
meinen Geschwistern mich, zu bewohnen deine Welt, sie zu heiligen mit Liebe, daß sie ein ewig angeschautes Denkmal werde—
zu bepflanzen sie mit unverwelklichen Blumen. Noch reiften sie
nicht diese göttlichen Gedanken—Noch sind der Spuren unserer
Offenbarung wenig—Einst zeigt deine Uhr das Ende der Zeit,
wenn du wirst wie unser einer, und voll Sehnsucht und Inbrunst
auslöschest und stirbst. In mir fühl ich deiner Geschäftigkeit Ende
—himmlische Freiheit, selige Rückkehr. In wilden Schmerzen
erkenn ich deine Entfernung von unsrer Heimat, deinen Wider-
stand gegen den alten, herrlichen Himmel. Deine Wut und dein
Toben ist vergebens. Unverbrennlich steht das Kreuz—eine Sie-
gesfahne unsers Geschlechts.

Hinüber wall ich,
Und jede Pein
Wird einst ein Stachel
Der Wollust sein.
Noch wenig Zeiten,
So bin ich los,

decorated them with colors and subtle shapes—or was it she, Love, who gave your jewels a higher, dearer meaning? What heaven, what pleasure does your life offer which outweighs death's delights? Doesn't all that inspires us bear the color of the Night? It bears you mother-like, and you owe all your magnificence to her. You'd evaporate inside yourself—you'd crumble away in endless space if she didn't hold you, tie you, so that you became warm and, flaming, sired the world. Truly I was, before you existed—my mother sent me with my brothers and sisters to inhabit your world, to hallow it with love, so that it would be a monument to look at forever—to plant it with flowers that won't fade. Still they haven't ripened, these divine thoughts— and still they are few, these traces of our revelation. Sometime your clock will show time's ending, when you'll become like us, and full of longing and craving you'll be extinguished and die. I feel in myself the end of your busyness—heavenly freedom, blessed return. In wild griefs I recognize your distance from our home, your resistance to the old, grand heaven. Your rage, your frenzy are to no purpose. The cross stands inextinguishable— our kind's victory banner.

> I quest over there,
> And each pain
> Will someday be a sting
> Of delight.
> In a few moments
> I shall be free,

Und liege trunken
Der Lieb' im Schoß.
Unendliches Leben
Wogt mächtig in mir,
Ich schaue von oben
Herunter nach dir.
An jenem Hügel
Verlischt dein Glanz—
Ein Schatten bringet
Den kühlenden Kranz.
O! sauge, Geliebter,
Gewaltig mich an,
Daß ich entschlummern
Und lieben kann.
Ich fühle des Todes
Verjüngende Flut,
Zu Balsam und Äther
Verwandelt mein Blut—
Ich lebe bei Tage
Voll Glauben und Mut
Und sterbe die Nächte
In heiliger Glut.

And lie drunk
In Love's bosom.
Endless living
Wells up strongly in me,
I look from above
Down here after you.
At that mound
Your splendor pales —
A shade brings
The cooling wreath.
O! Breathe me, Beloved,
Ravish me,
So I can pass on to sleep
And to love.
I feel death's
Rejuvenating tide
Transform my blood
To balm and ether —
I live by day
Full of faith and courage
And perish by night
In holy fire.

5

Über der Menschen weitverbreitete Stämme herrschte vor Zeiten ein eisernes Schicksal mit stummer Gewalt. Eine dunkle, schwere Binde lag um ihre bange Seele — Unendlich war die Erde — der Götter Aufenthalt, und ihre Heimat. Seit Ewigkeiten stand ihr geheimnisvoller Bau. Über des Morgens roten Bergen, in des Meeres heiligem Schoß wohnte die Sonne, das allzündende, lebendige Licht. Ein alter Riese trug die selige Welt. Fest unter Bergen lagen die Ursöhne der Mutter Erde. Ohnmächtig in ihrer zerstörenden Wut gegen das neue herrliche Göttergeschlecht und dessen Verwandten, die fröhlichen Menschen. Des Meeres dunkle, grüne Tiefe war einer Göttin Schoß. In den kristallenen Grotten schwelgte ein üppiges Volk. Flüsse, Bäume, Blumen und Tiere hatten menschlichen Sinn. Süßer schmeckte der Wein von sichtbarer Jugendfülle geschenkt — ein Gott in den Trauben — eine liebende, mütterliche Göttin, empor wachsend in vollen goldenen Garben — der Liebe heilger Rausch ein süßer Dienst der schönsten Götterfrau — ein ewig buntes Fest der Himmelskinder und der Erdbewohner rauschte das Leben, wie ein Frühling, durch die Jahrhunderte hin — Alle Geschlechter verehrten kindlich die zarte, tausendfältige Flamme, als das höchste der Welt. Ein Gedanke nur war es, Ein entsetzliches Traumbild,

> Das furchtbar zu den frohen Tischen trat
> Und das Gemüt in wilde Schrecken hüllte.
> Hier wußten selbst die Götter keinen Rat,
> Der die beklommne Brust mit Trost erfüllte.
> Geheimnisvoll war dieses Unholds Pfad,
> Des Wut kein Flehn und keine Gabe stillte;
> Es war der Tod, der dieses Lustgelag
> Mit Angst und Schmerz und Tränen unterbrach.

5

In times now passed there ruled over the far-flung races of people an iron fate with silent force. A dark and heavy blindfold lay upon their heavy soul—Earth was infinite—the gods' seat, their home. Since time unremembered its secret-filled structure had stood. Over morning's red mountains, in the heavy bosom of the sea, there lived the sun, the all-enflaming, living Light. An old giant carried the blessed world. Fast under the mountains the first sons of mother earth lay. Impotent in their destructive raging against the new rule of the race of gods and their relatives, the happy people. The ocean's dark green depths were a goddess's bosom. In crystal grottos an exuberant people revelled. Rivers, trees, flowers and animals had human sense. The wine poured by a visible fullness of youth—a god in the grapes—a loving, maternal goddess, growing upwards in full, golden sheaves—love's sacred intoxication a sweet duty to the fairest of god ladies—Life, like spring, thundered down through the centuries, an endlessly bright feast of heaven's children and earth's inhabitants—all races honored, child-like, the tender, thousand-fold flame as the highest thing in the world. Just one thought there was, just one atrocious dream image—

That, hideously, stepped to the festive tables
And wrapped the soul there in wild terror.
Here even the gods had no suggestion
How to fill uneasy hearts with comfort.
And this monster's path was full of mystery,
And no plea or gift could still its rage;
For it was Death who interrupted
This revelry with fear and dread and tears.

Auf ewig nun von allem abgeschieden,
Was hier das Herz in süßer Wollust regt,
Getrennt von den Geliebten, die hienieden
Vergebne Sehnsucht, langes Weh bewegt,
Schien matter Traum dem Toten nur beschieden,
Ohnmächtges Ringen nur ihm auferlegt.
Zerbrochen war die Woge des Genusses
Am Felsen des unendlichen Verdrusses.

Mit kühnem Geist und hoher Sinnenglut
Verschönte sich der Mensch die grause Larve,
Ein sanfter Jüngling löscht das Licht und ruht—
Sanft wird das Ende, wie ein Wehn der Harfe.
Erinnrung schmilzt in kühler Schattenflut,
So sang das Lied dem traurigen Bedarfe.
Doch unenträtselt blieb die ewge Nacht,
Das ernste Zeichen einer fernen Macht.

Zu Ende neigte die alte Welt sich. Des jungen Geschlechts
Lustgarten verwelkte — hinauf in den freieren, wüsten Raum
strebten die unkindlichen, wachsenden Menschen. Die Götter
verschwanden mit ihrem Gefolge—Einsam und leblos stand die
Natur. Mit eiserner Kette band sie die dürre Zahl und das strenge
Maß. Wie in Staub und Lüfte zerfiel in dunkle Worte die
unermeßliche Blüte des Lebens. Entflohn war der beschwörende
Glauben, und die allverwandelnde, allverschwisternde Himmels-
genossin, die Phantasie. Unfreundlich blies ein kalter Nordwind
über die erstarrte Flur, und die erstarrte Wunderheimat verflog in
den Äther. Des Himmels Fernen füllten mit leuchtenden Welten
sich. Ins tiefe Heiligtum, in des Gemüts höhern Raum zog mit

And forever, now, cut off here
From all that rules the heart in sweet delight,
Divided from the loved ones who inclined away,
Moved by vain longing and long sadness,
A languid dream seemed granted to the dead one
Only futile struggling imposed on him
The wave of pleasure—broken
On the rock of endless dismay.

With a bold spirit and high passion
Man beautified his gruesome worm,
A gentle youth turns out the light and rests—
The end is soft, like a harp's sigh.
Memory melts in the cool tide of shadow,
As the song goes, towards its gloomy need.
But a riddle remained unsolved—the endless Night,
The sober sign of a far-off might.

The old world neared its end. The pleasure garden of the
young tribe withered—out into freer, deserted space struggled
the no longer child-like, maturing people. The gods disap-
peared with their retinue—Nature stood alone and lifeless. An
iron chain held it in arid count and strict measure. Life's
immeasurable bloom fell off in dark words like dust and breeze.
Gone was the imploring faith, with its all-changing all-relating
divine twin, imagination. A cold north wind blew unfriendly
over the frozen plain, and the rigid place of wonders dissipated
into the ether. Heaven's distances filled up with glowing
worlds. Into the deeper sanctuary, into the soul's higher realm
the world's soul drew up with its powers—to rule there till the

ihren Mächten die Seele der Welt—zu walten dort bis zum An-
bruch der tagenden Weltherrlichkeit. Nicht mehr war das Licht
der Götter Aufenthalt und himmlisches Zeichen—den Schleier
der Nacht warfen sie über sich. Die Nacht ward der Offenbarun-
gen mächtiger Schoß — in ihn kehrten die Götter zurück —
schlummerten ein, um in neuen herrlichern Gestalten auszugehn
über die veränderte Welt. Im Volk, das vor allen verachtet zu früh
reif und der seligen Unschuld der Jugend trotzig fremd geworden
war, erschien mit niegesehenem Angesicht die neue Welt—In
der Armut dichterischer Hütte—Ein Sohn der ersten Jungfrau
und Mutter—Geheimnisvoller Umarmung unendliche Frucht.
Des Morgenlands ahndende, blütenreiche Weisheit erkannte zuerst
der neuen Zeit Beginn—Zu des Königs demütiger Wiege wies
ihr ein Stern den Weg. In der weiten Zukunft Namen huldigten
sie ihm mit Glanz und Duft, den höchsten Wundern der Natur.
Einsam entfaltete das himmlische Herz sich zu einem Blüten-
kelch allmächtger Liebe—des Vaters hohem Antlitz zugewandt
und ruhend an dem ahndungsselgen Busen der lieblich ernsten
Mutter. Mit vergötternder Inbrunst schaute das weissagende Auge
des blühenden Kindes auf die Tage der Zukunft, nach seinen Geliebten, den Sprossen seines Götterstamms, unbekümmert über
seiner Tage irdisches Schicksal. Bald sammelten die kindlichsten
Gemüter von inniger Liebe wundersam ergriffen sich um ihn her.
Wie Blumen keimte ein neues fremdes Leben in seiner Nähe.
Unerschöpfliche Worte und der Botschaften fröhlichste fielen wie
Funken eines göttlichen Geistes von seinen freundlichen Lippen.
Von ferner Küste, unter Hellas heiterm Himmel geboren, kam
ein Sänger nach Palästina und ergab sein ganzes Herz dem
Wunderkinde:

break of dawning world splendor. No longer was the Light the seat of the gods or their heavenly sign—over themselves they drew the veil of Night. Night became the mighty womb of revelations—the gods drew back into it—and fell asleep, only to go out in new and more splendid forms over the changed world. Among the people, who scorned by all had matured too early, and had become spitefully estranged from the blessed innocence of the young, the new world appeared with features never seen before—In the poverty of the poetic tabernacle—A son of the first Virgin and Mother—unending fruit of mysterious embrace. The orient's portentous, rich-blooming wisdom was the first to recognize the beginning of the new time—A star showed the way to the King's humble cradle. In the name of that far future, they honored him with splendor and fragrance, the highest wonders of nature. Solitary, the heavenly heart unfolded into a flower grail of almighty love—turned towards the Father's high countenance and resting on the lovely, earnest Mother's bosom that foreshadowed such glory. The blooming Child's prophetic eye gazed with consecrating fire onto the future days, looked upon His loved ones, the shoot of His god stem, unconcerned about His days of worldly fate. Soon the childlikest spirits of cordial Love collected around Him, wondrously seized by inner love. Like flowers a strange new love grew up in His presence. The inexhaustible word, the gladdest of messages, fell like the sparks of a divine spirit from His friendly lips. From far shores, born under Greece's happy skies, a singer came to Palestine and poured out his heart to the wonder-child:

Der Jüngling bist du, der seit langer Zeit
Auf unsern Gräbern steht in tiefem Sinnen;
Ein tröstlich Zeichen in der Dunkelheit—
Der höhern Menschheit freudiges Beginnen.
Was uns gesenkt in tiefe Traurigkeit,
Zieht uns mit süßer Sehnsucht nun von hinnen.
Im Tode ward das ewge Leben kund,
Du bist der Tod und machst uns erst gesund.

Der Sänger zog voll Freudigkeit nach Indostan — das Herz
von süßer Liebe trunken; und schüttete in feurigen Gesängen es
unter jenem milden Himmel aus, daß tausend Herzen sich zu
ihm neigten, und die fröhliche Botschaft tausendzweigig empor-
wuchs. Bald nach des Sängers Abschied ward das köstliche Leben
ein Opfer des menschlichen tiefen Verfalls — Er starb in jungen
Jahren, weggerissen von der geliebten Welt, von der weinenden
Mutter und seinen zagenden Freunden. Der unsäglichen Leiden
dunkeln Kelch leerte der liebliche Mund—In entsetzlicher Angst
nahte die Stunde der Geburt der neuen Welt. Hart rang er mit
des alten Todes Schrecken—Schwer lag der Druck der alten Welt
auf ihm. Noch einmal sah er freundlich nach der Mutter — da
kam der ewigen Liebe lösende Hand — und er entschlief. Nur
wenig Tage hing ein tiefer Schleier über das brausende Meer, über
das bebende Land—unzählige Tränen weinten die Geliebten—
Entsiegelt ward das Geheimnis—himmlische Geister hoben den
uralten Stein vom dunkeln Grabe. Engel saßen bei dem Schlum-
mernden—aus seinen Träumen zartgebildet—Erwacht in neuer
Götterherrlichkeit erstieg er die Höhe der neugebornen Welt—
begrub mit eigner Hand den alten Leichnam in die verlassne

You're the youth who since ancient days
Has stood in contemplation on our graves:
A comforting sign in the darkness—
A hopeful start to our new humanity.
What sank us into our deep down despair.
Draws us from here now with sweet craving.
In death eternal life is made known,
And you are Death who makes us whole at last.

The singer passed along, full of joy, to Hindustan—his
heart drunk with sweet love; and shook it out in fiery songs
under that glad sky, so a thousand hearts bent to him and the
glad tidings grew up thousand branching. Shortly after the
singer's departure that precious Life was the victim of the deep
human fall—He died young in years, torn away from his
beloved world, torn away from the weeping Mother and his
timorous friends. The lovely mouth emptied the dark grail of
unspeakable suffering—The hour of the new world's birth
drew near with shocking dread. It struggled hard with the old
fear of death—The pressure of the old world lay heavy upon
Him. Once more He looked fondly on the Mother—then came
eternal love's releasing hand—and he passed away. For only a
few days a deep veil hung over the surging ocean, over the
trembling land—the loved ones wept uncounted tears—the
mystery was unsealed—heavenly spirits hoisted the ancient
stone from the dark grave. Angels sat by the Sleeper—formed
gently from His dreams—Awoken into new godly splendor; he
climbed the heights of the newborn world—buried the old
corpse in the abandoned cave with His own hand, and set a stone

Höhle, und legte mit allmächtiger Hand den Stein, den keine
Macht erhebt, darauf.

Noch weinen deine Lieben Tränen der Freude, Tränen der
Rührung und des unendlichen Danks an deinem Grabe — sehn
dich noch immer, freudig erschreckt, auferstehn — und sich mit
dir; sehn dich weinen mit süßer Inbrunst an der Mutter seligem
Busen, ernst mit den Freunden wandeln, Worte sagen, wie vom
Baum des Lebens gebrochen; sehen dich eilen mit voller Sehnsucht in des Vaters Arm, bringend die junge Menschheit, und der
goldnen Zukunft unversieglichen Becher. Die Mutter eilte bald
dir nach — in himmlischem Triumph — Sie war die Erste in der
neuen Heimat bei dir. Lange Zeiten entflossen seitdem, und in
immer höherm Glanze regte deine neue Schöpfung sich — und
tausende zogen aus Schmerzen und Qualen, voll Glauben und
Sehnsucht und Treue dir nach — walten mit dir und der himmlischen Jungfrau im Reiche der Liebe — dienen im Tempel des
himmlischen Todes und sind in Ewigkeit dein.

Gehoben ist der Stein —
Die Menschheit ist erstanden —
Wir alle bleiben dein
Und fühlen keine Banden.
Der herbste Kummer fleucht
Vor deiner goldnen Schale,
Wenn Erd und Leben weicht,
Im letzten Abendmahle.

on it with an almighty hand which no power can lift.

Still your dear ones are shedding tears of joy, tears of affection and unending thanks at your grave—joyfully terrified, they still see you resurrected and themselves in you; see you weeping with sweet ardor at your Mother's bosom, soberly walking with your friends, speaking words as if plucked from the tree of life; see you hurrying full of longing to your Father's arm, bringing young humanity and the unspendable cup of the golden future. Your Mother soon hastened after you—She was the first to be with you in the new home. Long time's since flown, and in the higher and higher radiance your new creation stirred—and thousands draw near you out of pain and out of fear, full of faith and longing and loyalty—reign with you and the heavenly Virgin in the kingdom of love—serve in heavenly death's temple and are yours in eternity.

> The stone is lifted—
> Humanity is risen—
> We all remain yours.
> And feel no chains.
> The sharpest care flies off
> Before your golden basin,
> When earth and life give way
> At the last supper.

Zur Hochzeit ruft der Tod—
Die Lampen brennen helle—
Die Jungfraun sind zur Stelle—
Um Öl ist keine Not—
Erklänge doch die Ferne
Von deinem Zuge schon,
Und ruften uns die Sterne
Mit Menschenzung' und Ton.

Nach dir, Maria, heben
Schon tausend Herzen sich.
In diesem Schattenleben
Verlangten sie nur dich.
Sie hoffen zu genesen
Mit ahndungsvoller Lust—
Drückst du sie, heilges Wesen,
An deine treue Brust.

So manche, die sich glühend
In bittrer Qual verzehrt
Und dieser Welt entfliehend
Nach dir sich hingekehrt;
Die hülfreich uns erschienen
In mancher Not und Pein—
Wir kommen nun zu ihnen
Um ewig da zu sein.

Death summons to the wedding,
The lamps burn brightly —
The virgins stand in place —
There's no lack of oil —
If the distance would only sound
With your procession —
And the stars would only call to us
With human tongues and tone.

To you, Mary,
A thousand hearts are lifted.
In this shadow life
They would yearn only for you.
They hope to be delivered
With presentient desire —
If only you would press them, Holy Being,
To your true breast.

So many there are who were burning
Consumed in bitter torment
And fleeing from this world
Turned away then to you,
Who helpfully appeared to us
In many a need or pain —
We come now to them,
To be there forever.

Nun weint an keinem Grabe,
Für Schmerz, wer liebend glaubt.
Der Liebe süße Habe
Wird keinem nicht geraubt—
Die Sehnsucht ihm zu lindern,
Begeistert ihn die Nacht—
Von treuen Himmelskindern
Wird ihm sein Herz bewacht.

Getrost, das Leben schreitet
Zum ewgen Leben hin;
Von innrer Glut geweitet
Verklärt sich unser Sinn.
Die Sternwelt wird zerfließen
Zum goldnen Lebenswein,
Wir werden sie genießen
Und lichte Sterne sein.

Die Lieb' ist frei gegeben,
Und keine Trennung mehr.
Es wogt das volle Leben
Wie ein unendlich Meer.
Nur Eine Nacht der Wonne—
Ein ewiges Gedicht—
Und unser aller Sonne
Ist Gottes Angesicht.

Whoever, loving, has the faith
Weeps painfully at no grave.
Of love's sweet possession
No one can be robbed —
To soothe him in his longing,
And inspire him there's the Night —
His heart is guarded in him
By the faithful heavenly children.

Cheer then — life strides
Into eternal life;
Widened by inner incandescence,
Our sense is transfigured.
The starry world will turn into
The golden wine of life,
We will enjoy it
And be the light of stars.

The love is freely given,
There's no separation left.
The whole life billows on
Like an endless sea.
Just one night of ecstasy —
An eternal poem —
and all our sun's
God's face.

6

SEHNSUCHT NACH DEM TODE

Hinunter in der Erde Schoß,
Weg aus des Lichtes Reichen,
Der Schmerzen Wut und wilder Stoß
Ist froher Abfahrt Zeichen.
Wir kommen in dem engen Kahn
Geschwind am Himmelsufer an.

Gelobt sei uns die ewge Nacht,
Gelobt der ewge Schlummer.
Wohl hat der Tag uns warm gemacht,
Und welk der lange Kummer.
Die Lust der Fremde ging uns aus,
Zum Vater wollen wir nach Haus.

Was sollen wir auf dieser Welt
Mit unsrer Lieb' und Treue.
Das Alte wird hintangestellt,
Was soll uns dann das Neue.
O! einsam steht und tiefbetrübt,
Wer heiß und fromm die Vorzeit liebt.

Die Vorzeit, wo die Sinne licht
In hohen Flammen brannten,
Des Vaters Hand und Angesicht
Die Menschen noch erkannten,
Und hohen Sinns, einfältiglich
Noch mancher seinem Urbild glich.

6

"Longing for Death"

Down into the earth's womb,
Away from Light's kingdoms,
Pain's raging and wild force
Ensigns the happy departure.
We've come in from a narrow boat
Swiftly to heaven's shore.

Blessed be the endless Night to us,
Blessed the endless sleep.
Truly the day has made us hot,
And long care's withered us.
The wish for strange lands is gone away,
And now we want our Father's home.

What should we do in this world now,
With our own love and faith?
The old things have been set aside,
What use could any new ones be
O! There stands alone and in despair
Whoever deeply and truly loves the times gone by.

Those times gone by, where the senses' light
Burned brightly with high flames,
Where the Father's hand and countenance
Were still recognized by humanity,
And with high sense, in simplicity,
Many still matched to His former image.

Die Vorzeit, wo noch blütenreich
Uralte Stämme prangten,
Und Kinder für das Himmelreich
Nach Qual und Tod verlangten.
Und wenn auch Lust und Leben sprach,
Doch manches Herz für Liebe brach.

Die Vorzeit, wo in Jugendglut
Gott selbst sich kundgegeben
Und frühem Tod in Liebesmut
Geweiht sein süßes Leben.
Und Angst und Schmerz nicht von sich trieb,
Damit er uns nur teuer blieb.

Mit banger Sehnsucht sehn wir sie
In dunkle Nacht gehüllet,
In dieser Zeitlichkeit wird nie
Der heiße Durst gestillet.
Wir müssen nach der Heimat gehn,
Um diese heilge Zeit zu sehn.

Was hält noch unsre Rückkehr auf,
Die Liebsten ruhn schon lange.
Ihr Grab schließt unsern Lebenslauf,
Nun wird uns weh und bange.
Zu suchen haben wir nichts mehr—
Das Herz ist satt—die Welt ist leer.

The past, where still full blooming
And primeval races walked abroad,
And children, for heaven's kingdom's sake,
Yearned for pain and death,
And if also desire and life spoke,
Still many a heart broke from love.

The past, where with youthful ardor
God showed himself to one and all,
And with love's strength committed
His sweet life to an early death,
Did not avoid the fear and pain
Just so He would remain dear to us.

With anxious longing we see them now,
Shrouded in the dark of Night,
And in this temporality
Never will the thirst be quenched.
For we must go away to home
To know and see the holy time.

What holds us back from this trip home,
From our loved ones who have rested so long?
Their graves concluded on our lives' course,
We are sad, we are afraid.
We have no more to search for here —
The heart is full, the world is empty.

Unendlich und geheimnisvoll
Durchströmt uns süßer Schauer—
Mir däucht, aus tiefen Fernen scholl
Ein Echo unsrer Trauer.
Die Lieben sehnen sich wohl auch
Und sandten uns der Sehnsucht Hauch.

Hinunter zu der süßen Braut,
Zu Jesus, dem Geliebten—
Getrost, die Abenddämmrung graut
Den Liebenden, Betrübten.
Ein Traum bricht unsre Banden los,
Und senkt uns in des Vaters Schoß.

Endless and full of mystery
Sweet trembling courses through us —
To me it seems an echo sounds
Out of the deep distance of our grief.
Our loved ones too may be longing for us,
And sent to us this yearning breath.

Down now to the sweet bride, on
To Jesus, to the beloved —
Take heart, evening's darkling greys
To the loving, to the grieving.
A dream will break our fetters off,
And sink us forever in our Father's lap.

APPENDIX

(1)

Welcher Lebendige
Sinnbegabte
Liebt nicht vor allen
Wundererscheinungen
Des verbreiteten Raums um ihn
Das allerfreuliche Licht—
Mit seinen Strahlen und Wogen,
Seinen Farben,
Seiner milden Allgegenwart
Im Tage.
Wie des Lebens
Innerste Seele
Atmet es die Riesenwelt
Der rastlosen Gestirne,
Die in seinem blauen Meere schwimmen,
Atmet es der funkelnde Stein,
Die ruhige Pflanze
Und der Tiere
Vielgestaltete,
Immerbewegte Kraft—
Atmen es vielfarbige
Wolken und Lüfte
Und vor allen
Die herrlichen Fremdlinge
Mit den sinnvollen Augen,
Dem schwebenden Gange
Und dem tönenden Munde.
Wie ein König

(1)

What living person,
If any sense be gifted to him,
Does not love more
Than all the wonderful appearances
Spread out in space around him
The all-joyful Light—
With its beams and waves,
Its colors,
Its gentle presence,
In the day.
As life's
Innermost soul
It's breathed by the Giant-world
Of restless stars,
That swim in its blue tide—
The glittering stone
Breathes it,
The peaceful plant
And the animal's
So many formed,
Ever moved force—
Many-colored clouds and
Breezes breathe it,
And, above all,
The splendid strangers
With sensuous eyes,
With gliding gait
And with sounding mouth.

Der irdischen Natur
Ruft es jede Kraft
Zu zahllosen Verwandlungen
Und seine Gegenwart allein
Offenbart die Wunderherrlichkeit
Des irdischen Reichs.
Abwärts wend ich mich
Zu der heiligen, unaussprechlichen
Geheimnisvollen Nacht—
Fernab liegt die Welt,
Wie versenkt in eine tiefe Gruft,
Wie wüst und einsam
Ihre Stelle!
Tiefe Wehmut
Weht in den Saiten der Brust.
Fernen der Erinnerung,
Wünsche der Jugend,
Der Kindheit Träume,
Des ganzen, langen Lebens
Kurze Freuden
Und vergebliche Hoffnungen
Kommen in grauen Kleidern,
Wie Abendnebel
Nach der Sonne
Untergang.
Fernab liegt die Welt
Mit ihren bunten Genüssen.
In andern Räumen
Schlug das Licht auf
Die lustigen Gezelte.

As a king
Of worldly nature
It calls each power
To countless changes
And its presence alone
Bares the wondrous splendor
Of the earth's kingdom.
Downwards I turn
To the holy, unspeakable
The mysterious Night—
Over there, far, lies the world,
As if sunken in a deep vault,
How wasted and lonely
Her place!
In the strings of the breast
Deep sadness blows.
Memory's distances,
Youth's wishes,
Childhood's dreams,
The whole long life
Of short joys
And hopeless hopes
Coming grey-clad
Like evening mist
After the sun has set.
Far below lies the world
With its bright pleasures.
In other spaces
Light pitched
Happy tents.

Sollt es nie wiederkommen
Zu seinen treuen Kindern,
Seinen Gärten
In sein herrliches Haus?
Doch was quillt
So kühl und erquicklich,
So ahndungsvoll
Unterm Herzen
Und verschluckt
Der Wehmut weiche Luft?
Hast auch Du
Ein menschliches Herz,
Dunkle Nacht?
Was hältst Du
Unter Deinem Mantel,
Das mir unsichtbar kräftig
An die Seele geht?
Du scheinst nur furchtbar—
Köstlicher Balsam
Träuft aus Deiner Hand,
Aus dem Bündel Mohn.
In süßer Trunkenheit
Entfaltest Du die schweren Flügel des Gemüts.
Und schenkst uns Freuden
Dunkel und unaussprechlich,
Heimlich, wie Du selbst bist,
Freuden, die uns
Einen Himmel ahnden lassen.
Wie arm und kindisch
Dünkt mir das Licht,

Shall it never
Come back to its true children,
To the gardens
In its splendid house?
But what wells up?
So cool and refreshing
So forebodingly
Under the heart
And swallows up
The soft air's sadness?
Have you also
A human heart,
Dark night?
What are you holding
Under your cloak,
That grabs so unseen, strongly
At my soul?
You seem only fearful. —
Costly balm
Drips from your hand,
From a bundle of poppies.
In sweet drunkenness
You unfold the heavy wings of the soul,
And give us joys
Dark and unspeakable,
Secretly, as you are yourself,
Joys which let us
Sense a heaven.
How poor and childish
The light seems to me,

Mit seinen bunten Dingen,
Wie erfreulich und gesegnet
Des Tages Abschied.
Also nur darum,
Weil die Nacht Dir
Abwendig macht die Dienenden,
Säetest Du
In des Raumes Weiten
Die leuchtenden Kugeln,
Zu verkünden Deine Allmacht,
Deine Wiederkehr
In den Zeiten Deiner Entfernung.
Himmlischer als jene blitzenden Sterne
In jenen Weiten
Dünken uns die unendlichen Augen,
Die die Nacht
In uns geöffnet.
Weiter sehn sie
Als die blässesten
Jener zahllosen Heere.
Unbedürftig des Lichts
Durchschaun sie die Tiefen
Eines liebenden Gemüts,
Was einen höhern Raum
Mit unsäglicher Wollust füllt.
Preis der Weltkönigin,
Der hohen Verkündigerin
Heiliger Welt,
Der Pflegerin
Seliger Liebe.

With its bright things,
How joyful and blessed
The day's departure.
So now,
Since Night makes
Its servants strangers,
You'd sow
Gleaming spheres
In the far spaces
To show your Omnipotence,
Your return
In the times of your distance.
More heavenly
Than those flashing stars
In those far places we
Imagine endless eyes
Which the Night
Has opened in us.
Farther they see
Than the palest
Of all those countless hosts.
Not needing Light
They look through the depths
Of a loving soul,
Which fills a higher space
With wordless delight.
Praise to the world queen,
The high messenger
Of a holy world,
The guardian of blessed love.

Du kommst, Geliebte—
Die Nacht ist da—
Entzückt ist meine Seele—
Vorüber ist der irdische Tag
Und Du bist wieder Mein.
Ich schaue Dir ins tiefe dunkle Auge,
Sehe nichts als Lieb und Seligkeit.

Wir sinken auf der Nacht Altar
Aufs weiche Lager—
Die Hülle fällt
Und angezündet von dem warmen Druck
Entglüht des süßen Opfers
Reine Glut.

You come, beloved —
The Night is here —
My soul's enraptured —
The earthly day's past
And you're mine again.
I look into your deep dark eyes,
See nothing but love and bliss
We sink onto the altar of night
Onto the soft bed —
The veil is gone
And, lit by the warm pressure,
There glow the pure embers
Of the sweet offering.

[At this point in the *Athenäum* version the second section begins, and the
manuscript version, although mostly in verse, more nearly corresponds to it.]